U0928102

花与月光

英文名诗新译50首

[英]拜伦 等著

葛舒旸 等译

暨南大學出版社
JINAN UNIVERSITY PRESS

中国·广州

图书在版编目（CIP）数据

花与月光：英文名诗新译50首/［英］拜伦等著；葛舒旸等译. —广州：暨南大学出版社，2015.9

ISBN 978－7－5668－1627－6

Ⅰ.①花… Ⅱ.①拜… ②葛… Ⅲ.①诗集—世界 Ⅳ.①I12

中国版本图书馆CIP数据核字（2015）第219690号

……………………………………………………………………

花与月光：英文名诗新译50首

译　　者　葛舒旸 等

出 版 人　徐义雄
责任编辑　葛舒旸　黄圣英　冯琳
责任校对　颜彦
出版发行　暨南大学出版社（广州暨南大学　邮编：510630）
网　　址　http：//www.jnupress.com　http：//press.jnu.edu.cn
电　　话　总编室（8620）85221601
　　　　　营销部（8620）85225284 85228291 85228292（邮购）
排　　版　广州联图广告有限公司
印　　刷　深圳市新联美术印刷有限公司
开　　本　850mm×1168mm　1/32
印　　张　4.75
字　　数　80千
版　　次　2015年9月第1版
印　　次　2015年9月第1次
定　　价　26.00元

序

诗无达诂，是批评界的共识；译无定式，亦是译界的常识。尽管有“诗不可译”之忠告，一直不断有爱诗之人努力跃过语言和文化屏障，游向不可言传不可言尽的彼岸。根据个人读诗教诗兼及译诗的经验，我以为，译诗，特别是翻译抒情诗的工作，近乎示爱——向另一种语言示爱。

也许，这本精美的诗集可被视为一群花儿与少年的示爱。因欢喜一首他/她如此短如此美的英诗，而意欲将其化为汉语瑰宝。

最好的译诗总是留着译者的个性暗记，如穆旦之《秋颂》、飞白之《丽达与天鹅》、北岛之《秋日》，以至于读着它们的时候，我们往往以为原作者已经附身译者，用我们熟悉的语言、语调和韵律倾诉、蜜语、怨嗔、哀叹。显然，我们亦能从这本诗集里觉察一个译者与一首诗的感情会通、气质契合和文字缘分。至此，信、达、雅的翻译常规并不重要，更重要的是：爱上雪莱、爱上狄金森……并使他人分享自己的爱之愉悦；至此，“诗歌已死”的咒语不攻自破。

张箭飞

2015 年 8 月 10 日

前　言

我贪。欲以三五年华，二四韵句，去叩问深深沉沉幽幽远远的心曲。采短短吟咏，问山水无期，看西欧碧园，别意凄凄，欢曲款款。

我贪。欲集斯须少年，不怕天高，不惧地厚；不经流年，不问音律；以一脉执念，探万古曲章。

我嗔。古今相舛，西中语离。像那希腊朗俊，于碧海朝阳上迎风而立，湛蓝色眸子与天穹鸿水一色，清隽华永；水土与天成，心心念念，用江南墨色丹青，却画不出也描不对；水乡深浅小船，载不动，彼岸那流离大千世界的廊桥若梦。

我嗔。来往浮生，孜孜者有之，拳拳者有之，然经典彼山高远，千嶂依约浓云里，虽殚心竭力，亦无可登临。

我痴。诗若秋笛响起在暮山之上，层层清澈，句句婉转；如故人夜语，掩映在蓬庐水声里，笔笔笑容都是青山排闼，朗月照人。

我痴。我们不过小小少年，如何译得出经典？我不知。他们滂沱意气或依约心境，翻为二三句，转入我手，都细细推敲，辗转叩问。

我们知道，翻译的小小诗歌，经不起时光的碾压，经不起自己成长后若干年的眼光回望，可仍然要努力站在这里，要在时光的廓然大山里，留下汗水的一丝影子，留下心念的一点光晕。

我们在诗歌中看见水月洞天，于是，我们漂洋过海，用颤抖的翻译来轻轻叩问，花与月光。

葛舒旸
2015 年 8 月 16 日

Contents

目录

第一章

明月光，花影独酌

风往尘香，往日花影依约。
一款一曲，一念一动，一凝眸一垂首，
往事浓愁恣意，半圃落花无绪。
如一瓣寄怀，渺渺远山万里，
心无归处，青葱染枯枝。

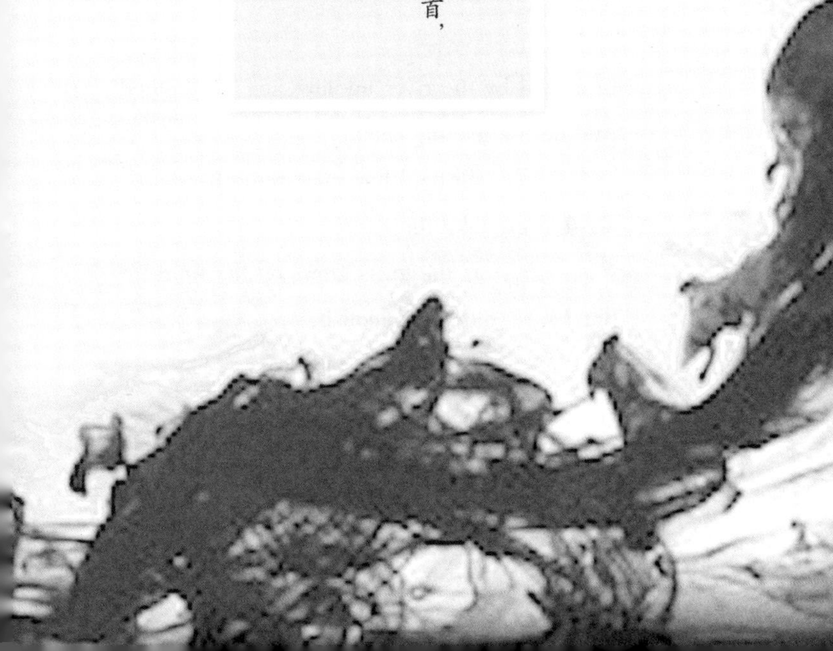

1 Down by the Salley Gardens

William Butler Yeats

Down by the Salley Gardens
my love and I did meet;
She passed the Salley Gardens
with little snow-white feet.
She bid me take love easy,
as the leaves grow on the tree;
But I being young and foolish,
with her would not agree.

In a field by the river my love and I did stand,
And on my leaning shoulder
she laid her snow-white hand.
She bid me take life easy,
as the grass grows on the weirs;
But I was young and foolish,
and now am full of tears.

1 游园惊泪

叶芝

花园深处，我与佳人相见；
她穿花拂柳而来，纤足如雪。
嘱我对爱一念清心，如枝上新绿泱泱；
而我年幼轻狂，岂肯轻易允诺。

河边曲野，我与红颜驻足，
她柔荑似雪，
轻依我肩。
嘱我对生活淡然处之，
如堤岸碧草茵茵；
彼时，
我年少愚顽，
而今，
热泪断肠。

2 The Sick Rose

William Blake

O Rose, thou art sick!
The invisible worm,
That flies in the night,
In the howling storm,
Has found out thy bed
Of crimson joy;
And his dark secret love
Does thy life destroy.

2 病恹之花

威廉·布莱克

玫瑰，你气若游丝！
隐形的虫，
在夜的飞沙走石里，
趁着摧枯拉朽的风暴，
与你夜雨对床。
他诡秘莫测的爱，
将你毁于一旦。

3 Roses

George Eliot

You love the roses—so do I. I wish
The sky would rain down roses, as they rain
From off the shaken bush. Why will it not?
Then all the valley would be pink and white
And soft to tread on. They would fall as light
As feathers, smelling sweet; and it would be
Like sleeping and like waking, all at once!

3 玫瑰吟诵

乔治·艾略特

你爱玫瑰——我亦如此。多期盼
空中朵朵玫瑰，落英缤纷，如那甘霖
轻拂过摇曳的灌木丛。为何不呢?
山谷的衣衫，或莹粉或柔白，
松软若毯，可款款漫步。花瓣摇落，
轻若白羽，香气清甜袭人；
一刹那间，似梦，似醒！

4 On a Faded Violet

Percy Bysshe Shelley

The odour from the flower is gone
Which like thy kisses breathed on me;
The colour from the flower is flown
Which glowed of thee and only thee!
A shriveled, lifeless, vacant form,
It lies on my abandoned breast,
And mocks the heart, which yet is warm,
With cold and silent rest.
I weep, —my tears revive it not!
I sigh, —it breathes no more on me;
Its mute and uncomplaining lot
Is such as mine should be.

4 凋逝罗兰

雪莱

花的氤氲已去，
就如，你的吻带给我的气息；
花的嫣然已去，
不再，明澈着独一无二的你！
空洞的壳，枯萎的躯，
缠绕着我荒芜的胸腔，
嘲笑着我冷热煎熬的痴心。
我哭泣，却唤不回它明眸善睐！
我叹息，却换不回它吐气如兰；
它的命运，缄默无怨，
恰如我的归宿。

5 Ah! Sunflower

William Blake

Ah, Sunflower! Weary of time,
Who countest the steps of the sun;
Seeking after that sweet golden clime,
Where the traveller's journey is done.

Where the youth pined away with desire,
And the pale virgin shrouded in snow.
Arise from their graves and aspire,
Where my sunflower wishes to go.

5 日光履者

威廉·布莱克

哦，向日葵！时光的疲倦者，
检点羲和的历履。
一路追逐金黄者，
在彼处，历历行路尽头。

彼处，青年耽于欲望而憔悴，
苍白的姑娘，深埋于皑皑大雪之下。
而他们都将从冥府醒来，
奔往向日葵的梦想腹地。

6 To the Moon

Percy Bysshe Shelley

Art thou pale for weariness
Of climbing heaven and gazing on the earth,
Wandering companionless
Among the stars that have a different birth, —
And ever changing, like a joyless eye
That find no object worth its constancy?

6 致月书怀

雪莱

你容颜苍白，
定是为孤悬天阙、凝望凡尘而倦，
流离于繁星之间，
孑然一身，无宿无眷，
如晦明不定、哀思绵延的眼，
凡尘俗世，是否，已不再值得你久久惦念？

7 Look Down, Fair Moon

Walt Whitman

Look down, fair moon,
And bathe this scene;
Pour softly down night's nimbus floods,
On faces ghastly, swollen, purple;
On the dead, on their backs,
With their arms toss'd wide,
Pour down your unstinted nimbus, sacred moon.

7 皓月惆怀

惠特曼

低头看看吧，明月，
来涤荡这遍野哀鸿；
把你的仙汁玉露，
倾倒给，游魂般浮肿的面庞，
倾倒给，断臂残躯、尸身不全的死者。
倾倒吧，圣洁的明月啊，
撒下你的灵丹妙药。

8 Moonlight, Summer Moonlight

Emily Brontë

'Tis moonlight, summer moonlight,
All soft and still and fair;
The solemn hour of midnight
Breathes sweet thoughts everywhere,

But most where trees are sending
Their breezy boughs on high,
Or stooping low are lending
A shelter from the sky.

And there in those wild bowers
A lovely form is laid;
Green grass and dew-steeped flowers
Wave gently round her head.

8　仲夏月光

艾米莉·勃朗特

月光，夏夜月光，
这般柔和、宁静、恬美；
中宵凝伫，
暗香浮动。

层层树木，向高处，
送着呼吸的柔枝。
或低垂纤腰，
向天空借处庇所。

在这无人打搅的林间，
月光蜕变了自己。
碧草如茵，
花露瀼瀼，
微风轻抚。

9 The Road Was Lit with Moon and Star

Emily Dickinson

The Road was lit with Moon and star—
The Trees were bright and still—
Descried I—by the distant Light
A Traveller on a Hill—
To magic Perpendiculars
Ascending, though Terrene—
Unknown his shimmering ultimate—
But he indorsed the sheen—

9 星月之途

艾米莉·狄金森

前路为繁星皓月所点亮，
树木明亮而静谧。
邈远幽光中，我看见，
山丘之上有位旅人，
沿峰峦叠翠，
扶摇着，翩然了尘世。
虽不知逐巅峰于何处，
他仍蕴蓄着熠熠之光。

与君書
如慕如泣

第二章

与君书，如慕如泣

与君书，叹不完浮桥三千段，数不清峰峦几万重。几时江南春又归，绿了平芜，飞了柳絮，灼灼了桃花，淙淙了流水。

与君书，人在迢迢青山外，书在殷殷寸心间。

与君书，几年离索，几许挂怀，凌乱不成言，歌如慕，意如泣。

10 "Why Do I Love" You, Sir?

Emily Dickinson

"Why do I love" You, Sir?
Because—
The Wind does not require the Grass
To answer—Wherefore when He pass
She cannot keep Her place.

Because He knows—and
Do not You—
And We know not—
Enough for Us
The Wisdom it be so—

10 与君书，我缘何爱你

艾米莉·狄金森

与君书，我缘何爱你？
因为
风并不向草索取答案
清风掠过
碧草便荡漾难安。

因他知道——而
你我所知不足
探开智慧所然

The Lightning—never asked an Eye
Wherefore it shut—when He was by—
Because He knows it cannot speak—
And reasons not contained—
—Of Talk—
There be—preferred by Daintier Folk—

The Sunrise—Sire—compelleth Me—
Because He's Sunrise—and I see—
Therefore—Then—
I love Thee—

骤然闪电——从不过问眼睛
光亮退后——他为何紧锁
因为他知道，不可言。
若置于言语，
因缘幻化千端。

若日出冉冉，
惊鸿一瞥，
油然，诚然，
付此爱慕。

11 How Do I Love Thee?

Elizabeth Barrett Browning

How do I love thee?
Let me count the ways.
I love thee to the depth and breadth and height
My soul can reach,
When feeling out of sight
For the ends of Being and ideal Grace
I love thee to the level
of everyday's most quiet need,
By sun and candle-light.
I love thee freely,
As men strive for Right

11 我如何爱你？

勃朗宁夫人

我如何爱你？
让我逐一细数。
爱得至深至宽至广，
直至灵魂边界，
直至存在尽头，
直至典雅消弭处。
我爱你，日日不可或缺，
不论日光熹微，不论烛光依约。
我爱你，以自由，
若追寻正义；

I love thee purely,
As they turn from Praise
I love thee with the passion
    put to use in my old griefs,
And with my childhood's faith
I love thee with a love
    I seemed to lose with my lost saints
I love thee with the breath, smiles, tears,
Of all my life! ——And, if God choose,
I shall but love thee better after death

以纯洁，

若笑辞嘉奖；

以往日悲怀里的心潮澎湃，

以咿呀童稚时的坚信不疑，

以对行将逝去的圣灵的亦步亦趋。

我爱你，直到一息尚存交出一生的笑与泪。

若上帝允诺，

在彼岸人生，我心如故。

12 Lines

Percy Bytsshe Shelley

1

That time is dead for ever, child!
Drowned, frozen, dead for ever!
We look on the past
And stare aghast
At the specters wailing,
Pale and ghast,
Of hopes which thou and I beguiled
To death on life's dark river.

12 光阴已逝

雪莱

1

光阴已逝，孩子。
溺于水畔，冻于冰原，永不再生。
我们回望往日，惊骇凝视：
你我沉迷的希望，
在生之暗流中，
渐无生意，
如幽灵哀泣，
苍白失色。

2

The stream we gazed on then rolled by;
Its waves are unreturning;
But we yet stand
In a lone land,
Like tombs to mark the memory
Of hopes and fears,
Which fade and flee
In the light of life's dim morning.

2

我们仍脉脉凝视的流水，汹涌若斯；

波浪一去不返；

我们却仍伫立

一隅孤地，

若累累墓碑，

铭住希望与恐惧的记忆，

在生命中某一个晦暗之晨，

目送他们褪色，悄然逝去。

13 Love and Friendship

Emily Brontë

Love is like the wild rose-briar
Friendship like the holly-tree—
The holly is dark when the rose-briar blooms
But which will bloom most constantly?
The wild-rose briar is sweet in the spring
Its summer blossoms scent the air;
Yet wait till winter comes again
And who will call the wild-briar fair?
Then scorn the silly rose-wreath now
And deck thee with the holly's sheen,
That when December blights thy brow
He may still leave thy garland green.

13 情与莫逆

艾米莉·勃朗特

怦然心动的爱慕，如野玫瑰的荆棘，
莫逆之交的友谊，如冬青树。
刺玫瑰嫣然之时，
冬青树仍苍色蒙尘。
然，谁能沁香久远？
孟春，刺玫馥郁，
仲夏，芬芳四溢；
而寒冬复至，
玫瑰何能傲霜斗雪？
笑弃那玫瑰花环吧，
簪上冬青光泽。
当十二月枯萎了你的眉目，
他仍留有，常青浣碧。

14 Love and Law

Vachel Lindsay

True Love is founded in rocks of Remembrance
In stones of Forbearance and mortar of pain.
The workman lays wearily granite on granite,
And bleeds for his castle,
'mid sunshine and rain.

Love is not velvet, not all of it velvet,
Not all of it banners, not gold-leaf alone.
'Tis stern as the ages and old as Religion.
With Patience its watchword
and Law for its throne.

14 爱与律令

林赛

真爱可见于记忆的巨石苍磊中，
在坚忍的石，与苦痛的囟里。
劳人筋疲力尽，于花岗岩上奄奄，
为他的城堡，鲜血淋漓，
无论烈日骄阳，无论骤雨骄风。

爱不是丝绒柔滑，也不尽是丝帛纤软；
爱不是标语，也不尽是金叶灿然。
爱，清俊如流年，亘古如宗教。
以耐心为暗语，以律令为冠。

15 Love's Secret

William Blake

Never seek to tell thy love
Love that never told can be;
For the gentle wind doth move
Silently, invisibly

I told my love, I told my love
I told her all my heart,
Trembling, cold, in ghastly fears
Ah! She did depart;

Soon after she was gone from me
A traveler came by,
Silently, invisibly;
He took her with a sigh.

15 秘密之爱

威廉·布莱克

莫要说爱，
爱无可启齿，
像那和风渐起，
无声，无形。

我倾吐我的爱，我呼号我的爱，
以醉生梦死的颤抖，以形销骨立的恐惧。
啊，她真的，不在了。

别后须臾，
旅人经过，
无声，无形，
以一声叹息，携她而去。

16 My Soul Is Dark

George Gordon Byron

1

My soul is dark—Oh! Quickly string
The harp I yet can brook to hear;
And let thy gentle fingers fling
Its melting murmurs o'er mine ear.
If in this heart a hope be bear
That sound shall charm it forth again;
If in these eyes there lurk tear
'Twill flow, and cease to burn my brain.

16 我心黯然

拜伦

1

我心忧矣——快，奏起那
急管繁弦，我姑妄听之。
纤手拂处，
若私语耳旁。
若心中尚缠绵一念渴盼，
伴着乐音，它将款款燎原；
若眼中尚噙有一泓泪水，
它将如雨坠落，不再苦灼我心。

2

But bid the strain be wild and deep
Nor let thy notes of joy be first:
I tell thee, minstrel, I must weep,
Or else this heavy heart will burst;
For it hath been by sorrow nursed,
And ached in sleepless silence long;
And now 'tis doomed to know the worst,
And break at once—or yield to song.

2

请狠狠地敲，深深地奏，

请深埋喜悦叮咚。

乐师呵，我只能以泪水致候，

只因我心沉沉，行将崩裂；

它几经悲恸，

长夜漫漫，辗转难安；

它劫数已至，

或一朝消亡——或在曲中醉生梦死。

17 Oh, They Have Robbed Me of the Hope

Anne Brontë

Oh, they have robbed me of the hope
My spirit held so dear;
They will not let me hear that voice
My soul delights to hear.
They will not let me see that face
I so delight to see;
And they have taken all thy smiles,
And all thy love from me.

Well, let them seize on all they can: —
One treasure still is mine, —
A heart that loves to think on thee,
And feels the worth of thine.

17 他们斩断，我的希望

安妮·勃朗特

他们斩断了我的希望
我念念珍重的期盼；
夺走，
悦耳如丝竹之音；
撕开，
寤寐辗转想念的面庞。
他们夺走了你的眉目含笑，
夺走了你的款款柔情。

罢了，让他们猖狂，
有一重念想永远是我的，
思君之心，
重如君意。

18 The Lover Mourns for the Loss of Love

William Butler Yeats

Pale brows, still hands and dim hair,
I had a beautiful friend
And dreamed that the old despair
Would end in love in the end:
She looked in my heart one day
And saw your image was there;
She has gone weeping away.

18 恋人惋叹

叶芝

黛眉纤淡，柔荑素静，乌发依约，
我识得一位娟秀红颜。
梦想着，旧日怨落，
终将涓涓逝于爱中。
一天，她望向我心中，
瞥见你的故影，仍宛然在斯，
她泣涕而去。

鼓樂起

第三章

鼓乐起，浮游遐思

袅袅歌吹，款款愁思；少年心事，簪花韵律。一夜闻笛，半漏萧瑟；如歌思慕，如诗叩问。恍若迢迢梦一场，遥遥影一重，惊醒了寒蛩，惊艳了浮生。

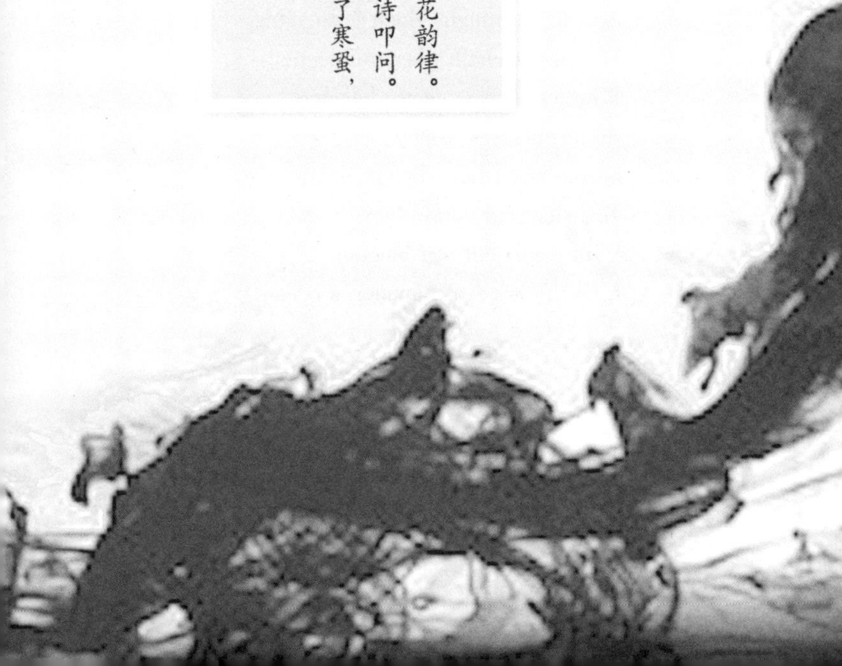

19 Stanzas for Music

George Gordon Byron

There be none of Beauty's daughters
With a magic like thee;
And like music on the waters
Is thy sweet voice to me:
When, as if its sound were causing
The charmed Ocean's pausing,
The waves lie still and gleaming,
And the lulled winds seem dreaming.

And the Midnight Moon is weaving
Her bright chain o'er the deep;
Whose breast is gently heaving,
As an infant's asleep:
So the spirit bows before thee,
To listen and adore thee;
With a full but soft emotion,
Like the swell of Summer's ocean.

19 钟鼓乐章

拜伦

无有美神之女，
神妙如你。
你的婉转莺啼，于我，
如水上泠泠轻音：
暂停了沧海，
波浪舒卷，溢溢杳渺，
和风渐息，恍然如梦。

午夜之月，
在深处舞若流光；
海的呼吸，
静谧如稚童酣睡：
灵，也为你折腰，
来听，来爱慕，
饱含款款之情，
如夏日海之潮汐。

20 Music, When Soft Voices Die

Percy Bysshe Shelley

Music, When soft voices die,
Vibrates in the memory;
Odours, when sweet violets sicken,
Live within the sense they quicken.

Rose leaves, when the rose is dead,
Are heaped for the beloved's bed;
And so thy thoughts, when thou art gone,
Love itself shall slumber on.

20 莺啼渐远

雪莱

当莺啼渐逝，
回忆绵绵，仍钟鼓萧瑟；
当芳葱病弱，
花香汩汩，仍沁然入扣。

玫瑰飞逝之时，
残叶砌成爱人的床；
你留下挂念，远走高飞，
独留蛰伏的爱。

21 Written for a Musician

Vachel Lindsay

Hungry for music with a desperate hunger
I prowled abroad, I threaded through the town;
The evening crowd was clamoring and drinking,
Vulgar and pitiful—my heart bowed down—
Till I remembered duller hours made noble
By strangers clad in some surprising grace.
Wait, wait my soul,
your music comes ere midnight
Appearing in some unexpected place
With quivering lips, and gleaming, moonlit face.

21 致音乐家

林赛

音乐，我拳拳渴慕于你，
怀此，我徘徊异乡，穿行市镇。
夜潮汹涌，喧嚣若斯，又迷醉若斯，
庸俗，可怜——我的心却卑躬屈膝——
直至我陡然想起，
是灯火阑珊处的惊鸿一瞥，
让碌碌无为的时光，飘然出尘。
静候吧我心，午夜前音乐将至，
在蓦然回首处，
唇瓣轻启，面庞如沐月光。

22 A Night Thought

William Wordsworth

Lo! Where the Moon along the sky
Sails with her happy destiny;
Oft is she hid from mortal eye
Or dimly seen,
But when the clouds asunder fly
How bright her mien!
Far different we—a froward race,

Thousands though rich in Fortune's grace
With cherished sullenness of pace
Their way pursue,
Ingrates who wear a smileless face
The whole year through.

22 月夜遐思

华兹华斯

天边一弯月，
欣然流转，
时常蔽于凡俗之眼，
或依稀难见。
而当彩云片片飞逝，
她多光彩怡人！
何其不同——刚愎自用的我们。

虽坐拥万贯家产，
仍耽于敛财。
碌碌经年，
愁眉难展。

If kindred humours e'er would make
My spirit droop for drooping's sake,
From Fancy following in thy wake
Bright ship of heaven!
A counter impulse let me take
And be forgiven.

若骨血的幽默，
终让我萎靡，
你随幻想幡然醒悟，
高瞻天际明船！
请宽宥我，
逆流而行。

23 Ode on Solitude

Alexander Pope

Happy the man,
Whose wish and care
A few paternal acres bound,
Content to breathe his native air
In his own ground.

Whose herds with milk,
Whose fields with bread,
Whose flocks supply him with attire,
Whose trees in summer yield him shade,
In winter fire.

Blest, who can unconcern'dly find
Hours, days, and years slide soft away,

23 孤居雅颂

蒲柏

福禄之人，
萦系，
几亩祖传薄田。
安心穷舍，
自由俯仰。

风吹草低见牛羊，
春摇麦田碧畦满。
匹匹棉帛，足以威裳。
郁郁林木，夏有荫，
冬有薪。

善莫大焉，蓦然回首，
年华迢迢远去。

In health of body, peace of mind,
Quiet by day.

Sound sleep by night;
Study and ease
Together mix'd; sweet recreation:
And innocence, which most does please
With meditation.

Thus let me live, unseen, unknown,
Thus unlamented let me dye,
Steal from the world, and not a stone
Tell where I lie.

肢体安康，神思清明，
昼日宁远。

夜长寐，
昼长读，
好读书，喜求解。
闲情漫溢，
以无知本真
参悟冥想。

我只是碌碌小人物，
来无兴者去无哀戚，
埋骨何须风水宝地，
石碑铭文不足道。

24 Sound and Sense

Alexander Pope

True ease in writing comes from art,
not chance,
As those move easiest who have learned to dance.
'Tis not enough no harshness gives offense,
The sound must seem an echo to the sense:
Soft is the strain when Zephyr gently blows,
And the smooth stream in smoother numbers flows;
But when loud surges lash the sounding shore,
The hoarse, rough verse should like the torrent roar;
When Ajax strives some rock's
vast weight to throw,
The line too labors, and the words move slow;
Not so, when swift Camilla scours the plain,
Flies o'er the unbending corn,
and skims along the main.
Hear how Timotheus' varied lays surprise,
And bid alternate passions fall and rise!

24 声思相扣

蒲柏

行文的安逸来自艺术，而非偶然，
娴熟的舞者，才能自在舞蹈。
不落痕迹，不惹纷争，
声音需像是感觉的回声：
柔和是微风轻抚的律动，
平静的溪流奏出更平静的乐章；
而当汹涌咆哮的巨涛撼动着海岸，
这声嘶力竭的狂野诗篇，化为那浪涛；
当战神奋力掷出巨石，
字里行间，举步维艰；
然而当敏捷的圣女搜尽旷野，
掠过挺拔的谷物，掠过广袤的大洋。
听，大师的乐音瞬息万变，
让情感多么惊奇，又跌宕起伏！

25 The World Is Too Much with Us

William Wordsworth

The world is too much with us;
late and soon,
Getting and spending,
We lay waste our powers;
Little we see in Nature that is ours;
We have given our hearts away,
A sordid boon!
This Sea that bares her bosom to the moon;
The winds that will be howling at all hours,
And are up-gathered now like sleeping flowers,

25 世界溢然

华兹华斯

世界溢然；
或迟或早，
我们将在予取予求中，
荒废力量；
眼前的自然不再为我们所有；
我们摒弃了自己的内心，
这不齿的福祉！
这与皓月交相辉映的大海；
这每一刻都在啸鸣的狂风；
此刻如同沉睡的花朵一般齐聚，

For this, for everything,
We are out of tune;
It moves us not. —Great God!
I'd rather be
A pagan suckled in a creed outworn;
So might I, standing on this pleasant lea,
Have glimpses that would make me less forlorn;
Have sight of Proteus rising from the sea;
Or hear old Triton blow his wreathèd horn.

对此物，对万物，
我们已离经叛道；
自然让我们纹丝不动——我的天！
我宁愿成为
一名信仰古愚信条的异类；
这样，我或许会站在这片欢愉的绿地上，
领略让我不至如此伶仃的风景；
或看见普罗透斯于海上升起；
或听见特里同吹响他的螺号。

26 The World's Wanderers

Percy Bysshe Shelley

Tell me, thou star, whose wings of light
Speed thee in thy fiery flight
In what cavern of the night
Will thy pinions close now?

Tell me, Moon, thou pale and gray
Pilgrim of Heaven's homeless way,
In what depth of night or day
Seekest thou repose now?

Weary Wind, who wanderest
Like the world's rejected guest,
Hast thou sill some secret nest
On the tree or billow?

26 浮世游者

雪莱

告诉我，星辰，你以光之翼，
烈烈燃烧，灼灼飞行。
在黑夜的哪处洞穴里，
你才肯卸下羽翼？

告诉我，孤月，你黯淡苍白，
浪迹无家可归的天堂，
迢迢朝圣。
何日何夜，
可言憩息？

疲倦的风啊，你漂泊不定，
似被全世界拒之门外。
你是否有一处幽密住所，
在寒枝头，在碧波中。

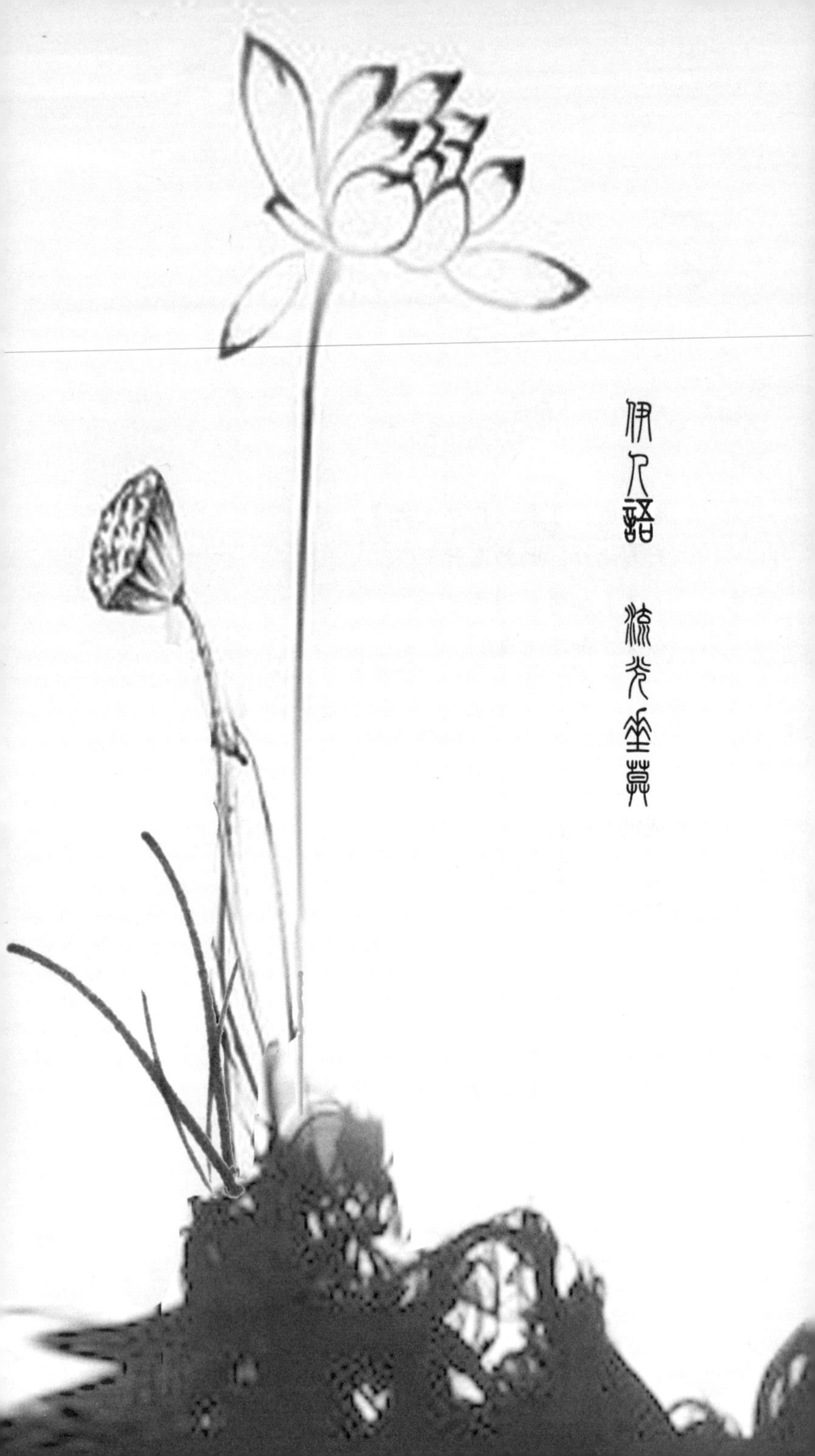
伊人语
流光坐莫

第四章 伊人语，流光垂暮

昼日长，流光短。伊人廊下，红颜舟中。眉梢，鬓边，喑哑的皱纹在凝眸，舒卷的腰身在顾盼。滴答，滴答，谁的光阴，临水照花，和远去的容颜频频絮语。

27 A Girl

Ezra Pound

The tree has entered my hands,
The sap has ascended my arms,
The tree has grown in my breast—
Downward,
The branches grow out of me, like arms.

Tree you are,
Moss you are,
You are violets with wind above them.
A child—so high—you are,
And all this is folly to the world.

27 少　女

庞德

树长进了我的掌心，
汁液沿着我的臂弯上溯，
树长进了我的胸膛——
俯身，
蔓蔓枝条溢出我的躯体，宛若臂膀。

你是碧树，
是青苔，
是风中款款摇曳的紫罗兰。
你是如此高昂的孩子，
而这一切，对这浮世，多无稽。

28 She Dwelt Among the Untrodden Ways

William Wordsworth

She dwelt among the untrodden ways
Beside the springs of Dove,
A Maid whom there were none to praise
And very few to love.

A violet by a mossy stone
Half hidden from the eye!
—Fair as a star, when only one
Is shining in the sky.

She lived unknown, and few could know
When Lucy ceased to be;
But she is in her grave, and, oh,
The difference to me!

28 孤 女

华兹华斯

她在僻静处，
溪流涓涓，圣洁不染。
不入红尘，
不惹爱恋。

她是紫罗兰，身影半露，
生苔的墓碑，影影绰绰；
美若孤星，
高悬夜空。

生，寂静无闻；
死，悄然无息。
孤眠黄泉的露西啊，
独我如此挂怀。

29 I Saw Thee Weep (Selected)

George Gorden Byron

I saw thee weep—the big bright tear
Came o'er that eye of blue;
And then, me thought, it did appear
A violet dropping dew:
I saw thee smile—the sapphire's blaze
Beside thee ceased to shine;
It could not match the living rays
That filled that glance of thine.

29 泣 女（节选）

拜伦

我曾见你哭——
眼珠湛蓝，泪水清幽；
真邪妄邪，
美似罗兰滴露。
我曾见你笑——
连城碧玉，
黯然失色，
难敌你倾国一瞥。

30 When You Are Old

William Butler Yeats

When you are old and grey and full of sleep,
And nodding by the fire, take down this book,
And slowly read, and dream of the soft look
Your eyes had once, and of their shadows deep;
How many loved your moments of glad grace,
And loved your beauty with love false or true,
But one man loved the pilgrim Soul in you,
And loved the sorrows of your changing face;

And bending down beside the glowing bars,
Murmur, a little sadly, how Love fled
And paced upon the mountains overhead
And hid his face amid a crowd of stars.

30 垂暮之女

叶芝

当你垂暮，白发苍髯，睡意昏沉，
昼日于炉火边，展书卷缓缓，
享阅读闲闲，梦昔颜款款；
临水照花时，目光若星辰；
姣好岁月里，得众人爱慕；
或情真意切，或逢场作戏。
唯独那人，爱着你，朝圣的灵魂，
爱着你，此去经年，老妪的忧伤。

于炽热炉火旁俯身，
幽幽悲诉，爱是如何飞逝。
消逝在群山之巅，
独留孤影，浩渺繁星间。

31 O Beauty, Passing Beauty! (Selected)

Lord Alfred Tennyson

O beauty, passing beauty! Sweetest sweet!
How can thou let me waste my youth in sighs?
I only ask to sit beside thy feet.
Thou knowest I dare not look into thine eyes.
Might I but kiss thy hand! I dare not fold
My arms about thee—scarcely dare to speak.
And nothing seems to me so wild and bold,
As with one kiss to touch thy blessed cheek.

31 红颜流暮（节选）

丁尼生

那女子，红颜流暮，
何忍让我，青春耽于叹息，
我仅奢求能坐于你脚边。
你知，我无勇气凝望你的眼眸，
又怎敢亲吻你的双手？我不敢
拥抱你——竟无语凝噎，
于我而言，无物似情狂，
触上你，天赐的容颜。

32 Memory

William Butler Yeats

One had a lovely face,
And two or three had charm,
But charm and face were in vain
Because the mountain grass
Cannot but keep the form
Where the mountain hare has lain.

32 流光记忆

叶芝

一人面如冠玉，
二三人风度翩翩，
而魅力和面庞都成空。
因为鬓山之上，
狡兔去后，
春草无痕。

33 The Past

Percy Bysshe Shelley

1

Wilt thou forget the happy hours
Which we buried in Love's sweet bowers,
Heaping over their corpses cold
Blossoms and leaves, instead of mould?
Blossoms which were the joys that fell,
And leaves, the hopes that yet remain.

2

Forget the dead, the past? Oh, yet
There are ghosts that may take revenge for it,
Memories that make the heart a tomb,
Regrets which glide through the spirit's gloom,
And with ghastly whispers tell
That joy, once lost, is pain.

33 往日时光

雪莱

1

记否，往日明媚时光？
曾被我们埋没在爱巢中，
尸体冰冷寒积，
花叶重重，不见霎阴，
花开花落，喜悦尽丧，
叶枯叶落，仍留一脉希望。

2

忘记死亡，忘记过往可好？
亡灵或许会寻仇，
心已沦为记忆坟墓，
追悔戚戚，愁云惨惨，
于耳畔细语，
欢愉已逝，而痛苦永恒。

34 I Wandered Lonely as a Cloud

William Wordsworth

I wandered lonely as a cloud
That floats on high o'er vales and hills,
When all at once I saw a crowd,
A host, of golden daffodils;
Beside the lake, beneath the trees,
Fluttering and dancing in the breeze.

Continuous as the stars that shine
And twinkle on the milky way,
They stretched in never-ending line
Along the margin of a bay:
Ten thousand saw I at a glance,
Tossing their heads in sprightly dance.

34 孤游若云

华兹华斯

我孤游若云，
浮沉山水间。
陡然看见，
大簇水仙，金黄若斯，
傍于湖岸，息于树下，
随清风，款款曼舞。

恒久似星辰，于漫天银河中，
熠熠照耀，闪闪眨动，
绵延不绝，
环绕湖湾；
一凝眸，便是千朵万朵，
摇头晃首，欢歌畅舞。

The waves beside them danced; but they
Out-did the sparkling waves in glee:
A poet could not but be gay,
In such a jocund company:
I gazed—and gazed—but little thought
What wealth the show to me had brought:

For oft, when on my couch I lie
In vacant or in pensive mood,
They flash upon that inward eye
Which is the bliss of solitude;
And then my heart with pleasure fills,
And dances with the daffodils.

波光粼粼，涌动于旁，
而花之舞，更欢欣；
丛花欢颜作伴，
诗人不乐而何？
我深深凝望，不曾顾虑
沉醉于此，是否换得累累财富？

当我独卧，
心境虚空，抑或郁郁寡欢，
她们总会惊鸿照影般出现，
用狂喜点燃孤独；
我心喜乐昭然，
随水仙翩翩起舞。

羅裙舞 一曲瀲灩

第五章

罗裙舞，一曲潋滟

舞舞舞，孩提手舞足蹈，少女心魂摇荡，智者生命铿锵，战士军舞歌彻。致每一曲心花怒放的潋滟，每一场山盟海誓的离愁别绪，每一篇泣鬼神壮山河的不归故事。

舞！舞！舞！

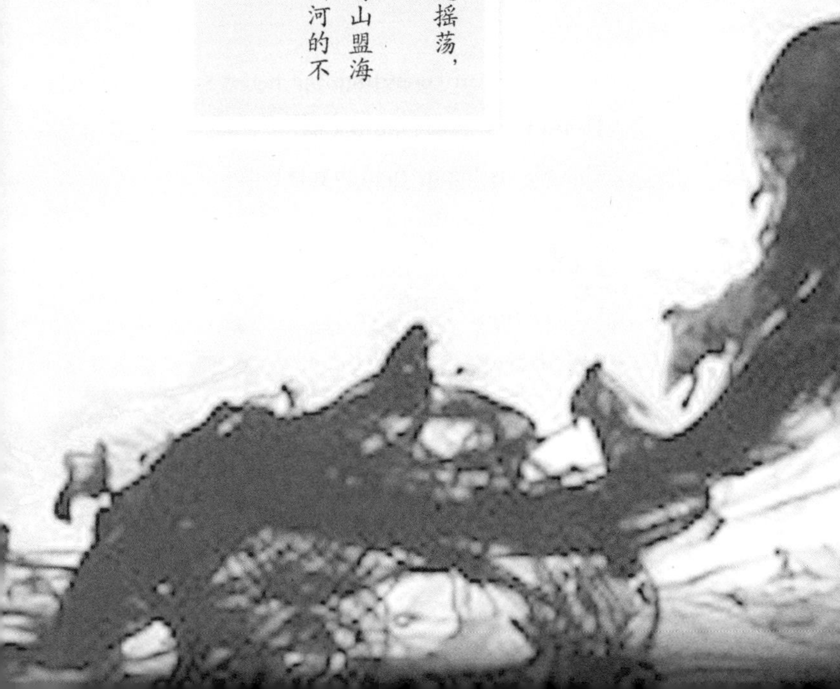

35 Sweet Dancer

William Butler Yeats

The girl goes dancing there
On the leaf-sown, new-mown, smooth
Grass plot of the garden;
Escaped from bitter youth,
Escaped out of her crowd,
Or out of her black cloud.
Ah, dancer, ah, sweet dancer!

If strange men come from the house
To lead her away, do not say
That she is happy being crazy;
Lead them gently astray;
Let her finish her dance,
Let her finish her dance.
Ah, dancer, ah, sweet dancer!

35 甜蜜舞者

叶芝

青草茵茵，少女曼舞；
稼穑告成，绿意萋萋。
花园夭夭，
抛却青春苦楚，
抛却世俗熙攘，
抛却乌云黑卷。
舞者，甜蜜舞者。

若有陌生男子顾盼，
携她而去，别说，
她恣于欢纵；
就让他们款款迷途；
就让她舞完这一曲。
舞，舞，舞，
嫣然的舞者。

36 To a Child Dancing in the Wind (Selected)

William Butler Yeats

Dance there upon the shore;
What need have you to care
For wind or water's roar?
And tumble out your hair
That the salt drops have wet;
Being young you have not known
The fool's triumph, nor yet
Love lost as soon as won.

36 风中舞蹈的孩子（节选）

叶芝

在高邈的海岸上舞蹈；
你应挂怀，
风的呼号，水的咆哮？
抑或是咸咸的潮湿水滴，
拨乱你的发？
年幼如你，并不明白，
庸人的胜利，并未知晓，
爱，甫一得到，便将失去。

37 There Is Another Sky

Emily Dickinson

There is another sky,
Ever serene and fair,
And there is another sunshine,
Though it be darkness there;
Never mind faded forests, Austin,
Never mind silent fields—
Here is a little forest,
Whose leaf is ever green;
Here is a brighter garden,
Where not a frost has been;
In its unfading flowers
I hear the bright bee hum:
Prithee, my brother,
Into my garden come!

37 天空在别处

艾米莉·狄金森

天空在别处，
永远碧蓝如洗。
阳光在彼处，
纵使黑暗阴霾。
离开凋谢之林吧，奥斯汀，
离开空寂山野。
这里，绿林虽小，
但枝叶常青。
有花园明媚，
永无阴霾。
在永不凋谢的姹紫嫣红中，
有蜂鸣如丝竹。
我的手足，请你，
来这碧园吧！

38 Answer

Sir Walter Scott

Sound, sound the clarion, fill the fife!
To all the sensual world proclaim,
One crowded hour of glorious life
Is worth an age without a name.

38 回答

司各特

吹吧！吹响那号角，吹响那战笛！
向所有的感官世界宣告，
宁要光辉岁月里，饱满的一时，
也不要碌碌无为中蹉跎的一世。

39 To You

Walt Whitman

STRANGER! If you, passing, meet me, and desire to speak to me, why should you
not speak to me?
And why should I not speak to you?

39 致　你

惠特曼

陌生人！如果你擦身而过，想与我说话，那么你，

为什么缄默？

而我为什么也迟疑着不开口？

40 On His Blindness

John Milton

When I consider how my light is spent
Ere half my days in this dark world and wide,
And that one talent which is death to hide
Lodg'd with me useless,
Though my soul more bent
To serve therewith my Maker,
And present my true account,
less he returning chide,
"Doth God exact day-labour, light denied?"
I fondly ask.

40 咏　盲

弥尔顿

无垠世界里，茫茫黑暗中，
还未曾历尽半世，我生之光，就已消耗殆尽。
小小庸才，埋藏与死亡无异；
而一念之灵，却屈膝祈望，
侍奉造物主，
献上我全部身家，
以免于责罚。
我愚顽疑惑："神要昼日长工，却永拒光明？"

But Patience, to prevent that murmur,
Soon replies:
"God doth not need
either man's work or his own gift:
Who, best bear his mild yoke,
they serve him best.
His state is kingly;
Thousands at his bidding speed
And post o'er land and ocean without rest:
They also serve who only stand and wait."

“耐心”横截了怨艾，
转瞬即答：
“上帝何需更夫劳力，
又何需凡俗供礼?
最能忍受苦厄者，
方最宜礼神。
他的国土若王庭，
号令一出，千人所指，
奔波于海陆山川；
纵使默立，虚怀等待，
也是献与他的致意。”

41 Eternity

William Blake

He who binds to himself a joy
Does the winged life destroy;
But he who kisses the joy as it flies
Lives in eternity's sun rise.

41 永 恒

威廉·布莱克

耽于逸乐且一味苛求者，
必痛失人生之翱翔；
随遇而安且一亲欣喜者，
方恒泽永世之朝阳。

42 Sonnet 12: When I Do Count the Clock that Tells the Time

William Shakespeare

When I do count the clock that tells the time,
And see the brave day sunk in hideous night;
When I behold the violet past prime,
And sable curls, all silvered o'er with white;
When lofty trees I see barren of leaves
Which erst from heat did canopy the herd,
And summer's green all girded up in sheaves
Borne on the bier with white and bristly beard,
Then of thy beauty do I question make
That thou among the wastes of time must go,
Since sweets and beauties do themselves forsake
And die as fast as they see others grow;
And nothing 'gainst Time's scythe can make defence
Save breed, to brave him when he takes thee hence.

42 十四行诗：当我数着报时的钟

莎士比亚

当我数着报时的钟，
眼见华丽的白昼陷入可怕的黑夜；
当我眼见紫罗兰渐渐逝去年华，
一头乌黑卷发也已被镀上斑白；
当我见到参天大树上的叶子皆枯萎，
它原是羊群纳凉之处；
夏季的植被也已被捆成一束一束，
带着坚挺的白须长眠于世；
我不免为你的美貌忧心，
它终有一天会随着光阴而逝；
幸福的事物固然稍纵即逝，
消于此处，又生于彼处；
万物皆逃不过光阴摧残，
唯子息新生令人们无惧于它。

蝶紛飛
浮生若夢

第六章

蝶纷飞，浮生若寓

暖意融融，阵风熏熏。
寒雪初融，草长莺飞。
蛱蝶戏舞，浮生斯虚。
似真似幻，长歌难语。

43 The Snow Is Melting

Kobayashi Issa

The snow is melting
and the village is flooded
with children.

43 冬雪正融

小林一茶

雪正融
村庄湮没在
儿童的叽喳里。

44 Butterfly Laughter

Katherine Mansfield

In the middle of our porridge plates
There was a blue butterfly painted
And each morning we tried who should reach the butterfly first.
Then the Grandmother said:
"Do not eat the poor butterfly."
That made us laugh.
Always she said it
and always it started us laughing.
It seemed such a sweet little joke.
I was certain that one fine morning
The butterfly would fly out of our plates,
Laughing the teeniest laugh in the world,
And perch on the Grandmother's lap.

44 蝶上笑语

凯瑟琳·曼斯菲尔德

粥盘之中，
绘着一只釉蓝蝴蝶。
每每清晨，我们都雀跃着，
盼着最先触碰到，那只蝴蝶。
祖母总说：
“不要吃那可怜的小蝴蝶。”
我们欢笑。
她总这么说，逗我们开怀。
暖心的小玩笑。
好似，
总会有那么一个明媚的清晨，
蝴蝶将轻扑羽翼，飞出杯盘，
带着世上最轻的笑语，
栖于祖母膝上。

45 The Butterfly

Louise Glück

Look, a butterfly. Did you make a wish?
You don't wish on butterflies.
You do so. Did you make one?
Yes.
It doesn't count.

45 蝶之梦愿

路易丝·格鲁克

看，蝶。是否有愿望？寄怀吧！
蝴蝶无法承载，你沉甸甸的祈愿。
而你当真祈拜。是真是幻？
是吧。
何必介怀。

46 A Poison Tree

William Blake

I was angry with my friend
I told my wrath, my wrath did end.
I was angry with my foe
I told it not, my wrath did grow.

And I watered it in fears
Night and morning with my tears;
And I sunned it with smiles
And with soft deceitful wiles.

46 浸毒之树

威廉·布莱克

我对友人心存怨怒：
和盘托出，不再芥蒂。
我对宿敌心有怨艾：
隐忍不言，怒火中烧。

朝朝暮暮，惴惴不安，
我以泪珠，豢养愤懑；
以温柔的言语，
欺瞒愤怒。

And it grew both day and night
Till it bore an apple bright.
And my foe beheld it shine
And he knew that it was mine.

And into my garden stole
When the night had veiled the pole;
In the morning glad I see
My foe outstretched beneath the tree.

它日夜膨胀，
结出苹果光芒熠熠。
我那宿敌见它芬芳闪耀，
明白那是我的。

夜幕笼罩大地，
我的宿敌悄悄潜进花园；
清晨，我发现
他僵死于树下。

47 A Lament

Percy Bysshe Shelley

O World! O Life! O Time!
On whose last steps I climb,
Trembling at that where I had stood before;
When will return the glory of your prime?
No more—Oh, never more!

Out of the day and night
A joy has taken flight:
Fresh spring, and summer, and winter hoar
Move my faint heart with grief, but with delight
No more—Oh, never more!

47 往日哀歌

雪莱

浮世！浮生！光阴！
我走到尽头，
故地伤怀，
青春的鲜妍何时归？
难难难！

欢愉飞逝，
不舍昼夜。
初春、盛夏、寒冬，呼啸而过，
以悲伤扰我心忧，而快乐呢，
罢罢罢！

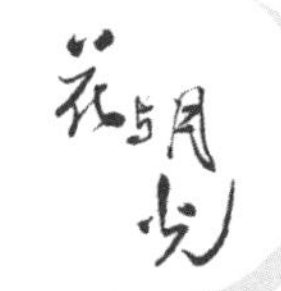

48 His Heart Was Darker than the Starless Night

Emily Dickinson

His Heart was darker than the starless night
For that there is a morn
But in this black Receptacle
Can be no Bode of Dawn

48 他心芜寂

艾米莉·狄金森

他的心，芜芜寂寂，比无星之夜还黯淡；

每一道墨色的黑夜尽头，总有瑰色的破晓将至；

而他的心，是深埋的，黑黢黢的罐子，

不见一丝将明之兆。

49 In This Short Life

Emily Dickinson

In this short Life
That only lasts an hour
How much—how little—is
Within our power

49 此生须臾

艾米莉·狄金森

此生短暂，
须臾即逝，
我们手中的权杖，
睥睨天下，又一无所有。

50 The Life We Have Is Great

Emily Dickinson

The Life we have is very great.
The Life that we shall see
Surpasses it, we know, because
It is Infinity.
But when all Space has been beheld
And all Dominion shown
The smallest Human Heart's extent
Reduces it to none.

50 不虚此生

艾米莉·狄金森

当下伟岸，
或然之生，
远超其上。
我们知晓，
因其无垠。
当寸寸土地都有归属，
当一切统治都已彰显，
小小的人，小小的心，
消于无形。

译后记

本书由中国浙江大学、武汉大学、暨南大学、上海外国语大学、香港中文大学，英国利兹大学，加拿大麦吉尔大学，澳大利亚悉尼大学，苏格兰斯特灵大学以及美国伯克利音乐学院、伊利诺伊大学厄巴纳—香槟分校、加利福尼亚大学欧文分校、罗切斯特理工大学、旧金山州立大学、爱荷华大学、路易斯安那州立大学等学校的硕士毕业生或在读学生完成。他们或是英语教学界的翘楚，或是金融、媒体等行业的中坚力量，或是学生中的佼佼者；他们散居世界各地，从事各行各业，相同的是对翻译的敬重、对经典的敬慕、对下笔的敬畏。

具体分工如下：王明宇2篇，其他参与人员，除笔者与黄秀外，每人1篇；黄秀联络数位同学，说明图书情况、担任指导老师；笔者承担组建翻译团队、选取英文诗歌、安排体例、翻译数篇诗歌及统稿工作。过程中所获帮助甚多，在此表示由衷谢意。

感谢众筹网提供的平台与帮助，助力传统出版多媒体融合与“互联网＋”，为图书宣传、销售模式提供了崭新思路和无限可能。

感谢武汉大学文学院教授、博士生导师、哈佛大学访问学者、资深翻译专家张箭飞老师，一路保驾护航，从译介与美学角度提供指导，并为本书作序。

感谢出版社领导和编校团队在出版过程中给予的大力支持和专业帮助；秉持“价值出版　文化传承”理念，以高效的团队协作和扎实的出版知识，为图书生产流程提供保障。

感谢译者团队中刘子扬、陆淳风、王文艳、仓宁忆、胡承祥、阳海涛、黄凯拍摄同名微电影；感谢魏泽军为同名曲作曲、编曲、录音，感谢邓子尧同学为本书绘制宣传画。

最后，感谢全体译者的诚挚付出，几篋短章，几番领悟，几许斟酌，文墨在凝神间，丹心在无声处；感谢诸位亲友及众多网友，对青年从事翻译的支持，对经典诗歌传诵的情怀。

葛舒旸

2015年8月16日

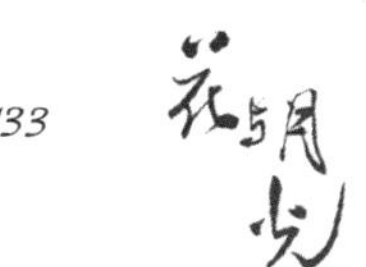